KV-013-235

This book
belongs to

Ean

Puddle's Fan Pages

Here's what other children have to say about their favourite puppy and his second adventure!

"It was so great I couldn't stop reading it till I got to the end! I hope there are more books about Puddle as I love dogs and would like to read more of his adventures." Sofia, age 7

"The story was adventurous and it was also funny. The funniest bit was when the Professor thought that Puddle was a robot dog! If you like funny books about magical adventures you will love this book. I am going to look for a magic puddle!" Ella, age 6

"Puddle is naughty and funny and brave." Hannah, age 7

"Ruby is clever. Puddle, I love you."
Ava, age 6

"I really like the bit when they jump into a puddle and just disappear like magic; it's so good." Florence, age 7

"The dog was so cute, I'd love one like that myself. The professor was funny with his words. I would really like to read another one of these books." Lydia, age 7

Toyshop Trouble

Puddle
the naughtiest puppy

Toyshop Trouble

by Hayley Daze
illustrated by Angela Swan
cover illustrated by Paul Hardman

A catalogue record for this book is available from the British Library

Published by Ladybird Books Ltd MMX
A Penguin Company
Penguin Books Ltd., 80 Strand, London WC2R 0RL, UK
Penguin Books Australia Ltd., Camberwell, Victoria, Australia
Penguin Group (NZ) 67 Apollo Drive, Rosedale,
North Shore 0632, New Zealand

1

Series created by Working Partners Limited, London WC1X 9HH
Text © Working Partners Ltd MMX

Special thanks to Jane Clarke

LADYBIRD and the device of a ladybird are trademarks of
Ladybird Books Ltd

This edition produced for The Book People Ltd,
Hall Wood Avenue, Haydock, St Helens, WA11 9UL

ISBN: 978-1-40930-903-1
Printed in England

For Eric and Janice,
great friends and neighbours

When clouds fill the sky and rain starts to fall,
Ruby and Harry are not sad at all.
They know that when puddles appear on the ground,
A magical puppy will soon be around!

Puddle's his name, and he's the one
Who can lead you to worlds of adventure and fun!
He may be quite naughty, but he's clever too,
So come follow Puddle – he's waiting for you!

A present from Puddle:

Look out for the special code at the back of the book to
get extra-special games and loads of free stuff at Puddle's
website! Come and play at www.puddlethepuppy.com

Contents

Chapter One
Amazing Discoveries

"Look at all these toys!" Ruby gasped. She and her cousin Harry were in Grandad's lounge, peering into an old toy chest. Ruby could see a jumble of model trains and aeroplanes, marbles and motorcars. They were the toys Grandad had played with when he was a little boy.

"What do you think that is?"

Harry asked, pushing his glasses up the bridge of his nose and pointing to a gleaming red-and-green object.

"Let's have a look," Ruby said, leaning so far into the toy chest that only her feet were sticking out. She moved aside a big wooden truck, a tank, and some small metal cars that got tangled in her long plaits. Then she grabbed the green-and-red toy and passed it to Harry.

"It's a clockwork train," Harry said, his eyes shining. At the front of the train was the engine, and there were three carriages behind it.

"It's the 2:15 from Paddington," Ruby said, "and Teddy is going to

visit Chips!" Teddy was Ruby's toy
duck-billed platypus. He had a long,
furry brown body, four big feet and
a beak like a duck's. Stitched to his
bottom was a new pink
tail Ruby's mother had
sewn on after a tug-
of-war accident.

Ruby sat Teddy on one of the carriages and Harry turned the key in the top of the train and set it on the carpet. It chugged across the room in the direction of Chips, Harry's toy robot.

"Go, Teddy!" Ruby said.

Tappety, tappety, tap. The train ran into a desk leg and ground to a halt, but the noise of drumming carried on.

Tappety, tappety, tap.

Ruby leapt up in excitement. "It's raining!" she cried, running to look at the raindrops pitter-pattering against the windows. Ruby could feel bubbles of excitement fizzing up inside her. The last time it rained, a little puppy called Puddle had arrived, and they had all been swept away on a magical adventure!

The back door blew open, hitting the kitchen worktop with a bang. A bundle of fur zoomed into the room like a rocket, knocked over the clockwork train, Chips and Teddy, and leapt into the toy box. It landed – *plumpf* – on the toys inside.

"Puddle!" Ruby shouted, clapping her hands with delight.

She and Harry looked inside the toy box to see a little puppy staring back at them. His pink tongue was lolling out and his white tail wagged happily.

Harry patted Puddle on the head. "I'd forgotten what a naughty puppy he is."

"He's pretending to be a toy!" Ruby said, laughing. She scooped him up in her arms. "He's definitely as cuddly as Teddy."

"Woof! Woof!" barked Puddle, as if he agreed. Then he wriggled free, dashed across the room, through the kitchen, and into the rainy garden.

"Come on!" Ruby shouted with excitement. They rushed after him.

Outside, Puddle bounded down the garden path, splashing in the puddles. His tail was wagging so hard that a blur of raindrops sprayed out. Ruby

held out her hands to catch some of
the sparkling drops. From behind his
glasses, Harry's eyes were shining.

Puddle stopped in front of a particularly large pool of water and raced around and around it. The raindrops were making the surface ripple and shimmer. He crouched down, then jumped into the water with a splash – and disappeared right through the puddle. Just like last time.

Ruby grinned at Harry. "Are you ready for our next adventure?" she asked.

"What if the magic doesn't work today?" Harry asked. "The likelihood of another magic puddle is very low."

"We won't know until we try," Ruby said. "One, two, three – JUMP!"

And they leapt into the puddle.

Chapter Two

The Puppy and the Professor

Ruby found herself in complete darkness, surrounded by soft, fluffy objects.

"Puddle," Ruby called, "where are you?"

Puddle gave a yip.

"I've never seen a Robodog toy before," said a loud, deep voice. "He looks so amaze-errifically real!"

"What's happening?" Harry whispered from somewhere next to Ruby.

"I don't know," she said, "but we need to get out of here!"

She and Harry wriggled their way upwards through the soft objects. Light began to seep through. Ruby pushed aside a cuddly dinosaur – and realized that they were inside a huge toy box. It was even bigger than Grandad's. The toy box was inside a large room with high ceilings. Shelves lined the walls, and they were bursting with every kind of toy Ruby could imagine – teddy bears, jigsaws, electronic games and train sets. Long

ladders were fixed to the shelves, and
people in red aprons were climbing
up them, putting more wonderful
toys on display. There was a cash
register at the front of the room.

"Look!" Harry pointed to a sign written in enormous sparkly letters, high up on the wall.

"Gigglesworth Toys," Ruby read. "We're inside a huge toyshop!"

"And there's Puddle," Harry said, his forehead wrinkled with worry.

The little puppy was tucked under the arm of a tall man in a white lab coat. He was carrying a box with the other arm. "Brill-ificent," the man said, looking down at Puddle. "I must find out how to make one of these."

"He thinks Puddle's a toy," Harry gasped.

"We're coming, Puddle!" Ruby called.

She and Harry scrambled out of
the enormous toy box. When Puddle
saw them, he squirmed out from the
man's arm and scampered under his
feet – tripping the man over.

Crash! The man's box went flying. All sorts of odds and ends rolled across the floor.

"Oh, dearie me!" the man exclaimed, running his hands through his spiky white hair. Then he looked at Puddle. "You're not a Robodog, are you?"

"Puddle's real," Ruby said, smiling. "He can be rather naughty sometimes. We'll help you tidy up."

She knelt down, gathering the
cotton reels, ribbon, string and
shiny buttons. Beside her, Harry
was collecting nuts and bolts and
an electronic circuit board. Puddle
ran to greet Ruby and Harry. When
the man patted his head,
Puddle dropped a pot of
glue by the man's feet.

33

"You didn't mean to make a mess, did you, Puddle?" said the man. "I'm Professor Toyjoy," he added, shaking Ruby and Harry by the hand and Puddle by the paw.

"I'm Ruby," Ruby said, "and this is my cousin, Harry. What are these things?" she asked the professor as he repacked his box.

"My fixi-mend kit," the professor replied. "I can't get the thing-gummy-bobby to work. Nothing works today!"

"Perhaps we can help fix the thing-gummy-bobby," Harry said, "if you tell us what it is."

"That's wondrously kind, but thing-gummy-bobbies have to be kept hush-hush," Professor Toyjoy told them, closing the box. "What a day!" he murmured. He looked at his watch. "I have to get to work. Time's zippety-zipping away."

Professor Toyjoy backed hastily through the swing doors at the back of the toyshop.

Ruby saw that Puddle was nosing
at something behind the toy box.
"What have you got there?" she
wondered, taking the object from
Puddle's mouth.

"It's a kind of screwdriver," said Harry. He pressed the button on its side, and the screwdriver whirred round. Red and blue lights flashed on its handle. "I've never seen one like this before. It must have fallen out of the professor's box."

Ruby hurried over to the swing doors. "We need to find him and give it back!"

Chapter Three
Top Secret Toys

Ruby, Harry and Puddle pushed
through the swing doors and into a
long, twisting corridor. It was empty.

"Where's the professor?" Ruby
asked.

The corridor was lined with open
doors. Ruby and Harry peered inside
the first one and saw two women in white
lab coats, sawing out jigsaw pieces.

"They're making toys for the shop," Harry whispered.

"Maybe the professor's in one of these rooms," Ruby suggested.

Through each door they saw all sorts of toys – boxed games, computer games, toys with batteries, toys with wheels. There was a whole room of aeroplanes, another of trains and one of princess dolls dressed in pink. In another room, a man was pumping up brightly coloured beach balls and stacking them in a neat pyramid.

Puddle wagged his tail and trotted inside. He batted one of the balls with his paw, making it bounce

around the room. Ruby ran over and
steadied the wobbling beach ball
pyramid.

"We're very sorry," she said to
the man. "Puddle didn't mean to be
naughty – he just wants to play."

But the man was grinning. "That's
what these beach balls are for!" He
tickled Puddle's ears.

"Have you seen Professor Toyjoy?" Harry asked.

Before the man could reply, Puddle yapped loudly and scampered back into the corridor, his paws pattering against the tiles. Ruby ran out and saw the back of a spiky white head. The professor was walking towards another set of swing doors at the end of the corridor.

"Professor Toyjoy!" Ruby called.

But the professor had already gone through. Above the doors was a sign that said: INVENTORS AT WORK. TOP SECRET.

"Do you think we're allowed to go inside?" Harry wondered.

Ruby looked down at the screwdriver in her hand. "The professor won't be able to mend anything if we don't," she said.

Puddle barked his agreement, and pushed the doors open with his nose.

The other side of the doors
reminded Ruby of a giant classroom.
It was full of men and women in lab

coats bent over their workbenches. There were wires and microchips, circuit boards, computer screens, switches and batteries scattered everywhere.

"It's a laboratory! They must all be toy inventors," Harry whispered, clearly amazed by it all. "I'd like to be an inventor."

Ruby looked around the room. "But where's Professor Toyjoy gone? I can't see..."

But as she spoke, from the back of the workshop there came a bright flash of light and a huge...
...*BANG!*

Chapter Four
The Supertronic
Starblaster

Harry and Ruby ducked under the closest bench as a shower of sparkly silver dust rained down on the workshop. Puddle hid his eyes with his paws.

"Professor Toyjoy's exploding things again," a woman said, wiping glitter from her brow. "At least it's only glitter this time. Last week it was glue, and we were all stuck to the floor."

"Puddle, Harry! Come on!" Ruby scrambled out from under the workbench and raced to the back of the workshop.

The professor was standing in a heap of gently smoking machine parts, shaking his head.

"Dearie me," he muttered, rummaging through his fixi-mend kit. "That's the end of the Supertronic Starblaster. And I'll never fix it without my –"

"Is this what you're looking for?" Ruby asked him. She leapt over a pool of silver goo and held out the screwdriver.

"Gracious me!" the professor said, beaming at them. "Thank you!"

But then his smile faded as he looked at his watch.

"Is something the matter?" Ruby asked him. Puddle slithered about in the silver goo and pattered silvery paw prints across the floor.

"I'm just a trifle flusterous," he said, running his hands through his hair. "Mr Gigglesworth will be here soon to judge the competition."

"What competition?" Harry asked, prodding what looked like a heap of crumpled-up tinfoil that had been grilled on a barbecue. Puddle growled as it fell over.

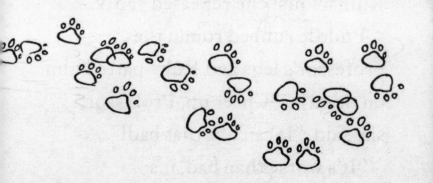

"Mr Gigglesworth's competition," Professor Toyjoy told them. "The competition to find a new bestselling toy for Gigglesworth Toys." He sighed. "The Supertronic Starblaster was my best hope. I designed it to shoot glitteroid stars to stick on children's bedroom ceilings. But it blasted itself, and now everything is ruinacious. Ruinacious!" he repeated sadly.

Puddle rubbed round the professor's legs and Ruby patted him on the arm. "Cheer up, Professor," she said. "It can't be that bad!"

"It's worse than bad, it's horribloid!" the professor groaned.

"You see, every toy inventor has to create a toy for Mr Gigglesworth's competition. And these days, all that kids want are computer gadgets and thing-gummy-bobbies with batteries . . ."

"Like my robot, Chips," Harry agreed.

Professor Toyjoy nodded, then pointed to his workbench. It was covered in a red cloth that was draped over strange lumps and bumps and sprinkled with silver glitter.

"I've got some fantabulous thing-gummy-bobbies under there," the professor said, "but none of them work." The professor sat down on his chair and put his head in his hands. "I've been inventing toys for forty years," he mumbled. "I don't want to lose my job. It's the most marvel-tastic job-erino in the world!"

Puddle jumped up on the professor's lap and nudged him sympathetically with his nose.

Ruby looked at Harry. He nodded, as if he knew exactly what she was thinking. "Let's help!" she exclaimed.

Chapter Five
Toy Trouble

"Woof! Woof!" Puddle pulled off
the red cloth covering the professor's
workbench. Glitter settled like
snow as Ruby rolled up her sleeves.
Under the red cloth was a jumble of
peculiar-looking toys.

Harry picked up a toy snowman
with an upside-down head. "What
are these things?" Harry asked

Professor Toyjoy.

The professor looked up. "These watcha-ma-bits? They're all floppers," he sighed, absent-mindedly stroking Puddle's soft ears. "Toys that didn't work."

"Maybe we can help fix one of them," Ruby said eagerly. "Harry's good at fixing things, and I've got lots of ideas."

"I suppose it's worth a try," Professor Toyjoy said. Puddle leapt to the floor as the professor got to his feet and picked up a toy from his workbench. "How about this one – the Whopping Whale Everlasting Bubble Maker," the professor said, pointing to a football-sized machine shaped like a whale with an open mouth.

"What's wrong with it?" Ruby asked.

"I designed it so the everlasting bubbles can be used as balls," Professor Toyjoy said, pouring a cupful of what looked like bright green slime into the whale's mouth. "But the bubble mix is a trifle unrightful . . ."

They watched open-mouthed as bright green bubbles the size of tennis balls shot out of the whale's blowhole. Puddle jumped up and caught one.

Pop! Puddle yelped with surprise. His nose was splattered with green goo.

Pop! Pop! Pop! Ruby jumped out of the way as the other bubbles burst,

spattering green slime everywhere.

"Yuck!" Harry wiped the sticky green ooze off his glasses. "I'd need to look at my chemistry books to help you get that mix right. We don't have time for that right now."

Ruby pointed to something that looked like a plastic toy cat sitting on top of a clay machine.

"Perhaps we can make this toy work," she said hopefully.

"It's a Copy Cat," Professor

Toyjoy explained enthusiastically. "You put different-coloured clay in the machine, and scan your favourite toy with the scantastic scanner, then the Copy Cat computer gadget tells the machine to make an exact copy of the toy."

"Then you can have twice as much fun!" Harry said.

"That's the idea." The professor sighed. "But it isn't quite correctish yet ..." He switched on the Copy Cat and handed what looked like a TV remote control to Ruby.

"Let's try it!" Ruby said, running the scanner over the Whopping Whale Everlasting Bubble Maker.

A multicoloured clay snake oozed
out of the machine.

"Grrrr!" Puddle growled, grabbing

the snake and wrestling with it on the floor.

Ruby giggled. "These are all fabulous watcha-ma-bobbies!" she told the professor.

"But we don't have time to repair-inate them!" Professor Toyjoy groaned.

"Then we'll just have to invent something new!" Ruby said.

Ruby closed her eyes tight and screwed up her freckly face in concentration. What new toy could they invent?

Chapter Six
The Amaze-errific New Toy

"Woof! Woof! Woof!"

"Puddle!" Ruby cried. "What's the matter?" She opened her eyes and looked around for the puppy.

He was in the corner of the workshop, right next to an old toy chest. She hurried over, closely followed by Harry and Professor Toyjoy.

Puddle was scratching at the wooden box, as if he was trying to dig his way into it.

Harry shook his head. "Don't be naughty, Puddle," he said.

"I don't think he's being naughty," Ruby said. "He wants us to look inside."

Puddle wagged his tail as Ruby lifted the lid.

"Ooh!" Ruby gasped in delight. The box was full of lovely soft toys. "Look what Puddle's found," she said to Harry and the professor. "Good boy, Puddle!"

Puddle scrambled into the box. He dived into the toys, and when he emerged again he had one in his mouth. It was a beautiful rainbow-coloured parrot, with only one wing. Ruby took it and gave it a hug. Its feathers were silky. *What a shame it's damaged*, she thought.

Puddle buried himself again and passed Ruby more toys. There was a friendly-looking furry red dragon that was missing a tail, a plump velvety bunny without any ears and a yellow-and-black stripy bumblebee with an unstuffed tummy and no antennae. Ruby cuddled each one as he pulled them out. They all looked brand new.

"What's at the bottom, Puddle?" she asked.

Ruby dived head first into the box. She felt around in the darkness. The bottom of the chest was littered with the missing pieces. She stood up clutching them in her arms.

"Don't bother with those old-fangled things," Professor Toyjoy said. "They're unfinished try-it-outs. When I first came to work for

Gigglesworth Toys, I designed soft toys. That's not the sort of thing Mr Gigglesworth wants now, even if they are splendiferously cuddleful."

73

"Splendiferously cuddleful," Ruby repeated. She thought of Teddy, her duck-billed platypus, with his pink tail, duck's beak and big feet ...

Ruby's plaits swung as she whirled round. "I've got an idea!" she squealed. Soft toys pattered on to the floor as she climbed out of the toy box. "We can use these parts to make a new toy. If everyone else is making gadgets and computer games, a strange and wonderful cuddly toy is sure to stand out."

"An entirely new crazy cuddly creature ..." Harry said slowly. "It might work."

"That's its name!" Ruby exclaimed

excitedly. "Crazy Cuddly Creature!" Puddle yapped and wagged his tail. "See, Puddle agrees!"

The professor beamed at them. "So do I. That sounds superfantastical!"

He turned to Puddle and patted his head. "Go on, Puddle," he said. "Fetch the pieces!"

Puddle leapt back into the toy chest and rummaged enthusiastically through the try-it-out toys. He emerged with a round, purple shape and passed it to Ruby.

"This can be the toy's head," she decided.

Puddle dived back into the toy chest and reappeared with two long, fuzzy pipe cleaners.

"And these are its antennae," Harry said.

Professor Toyjoy clapped his hands. "Now, where's my screwdriver?"

Puddle pulled more pieces from the toy chest, and Ruby and Harry decided what part of the toy each piece would be, holding them in place while Professor Toyjoy fitted their creation together.

In no time at all, the creature was nearly finished. Ruby thought it looked amaze-eriffic. It was the size of a big teddy bear, and as well as its antennae, it had bright blue buttons for eyes, bunny ears, whiskers on its nose, parrot's wings, a dragon's tail and feet, and a fat bumblebee-striped tummy. It even had a pouch on its front that held a little bear.

Ruby just couldn't help smiling when she looked at it. It was a perfect Crazy Cuddly Creature.

"Mr Gigglesworth is in the toyshop!" a loudspeaker announced, just as Professor Toyjoy finished

attaching the creature's tail.
"Toymakers! It's time to present
your toys!"

Chapter Seven
Competition Time

Puddle's furry head poked out of the toy chest. He had a long blue ribbon in his mouth.

"Well done, Puddle," Ruby said. "That's the finishing touch." She quickly tied a colourful bow round the Crazy Cuddly Creature's neck and thrust it into Professor Toyjoy's arms. She tugged on her plaits for luck and wished as hard as she could that Mr Gigglesworth would like the Crazy Cuddly Creature as much as she did.

All around them, the other toy inventors were scurrying to grab their whizzing, bleeping creations and line up in front of their workbenches. Professor Toyjoy regarded them with dismay.

"Oh dearie me," he groaned. "Look at all those whizz-bang inventions. I can't show Mr Gigglesworth a soft toy. It doesn't do anything."

Ruby and Harry looked at each other in horror as Mr Toyjoy pushed the Crazy Cuddly Creature into the

toy chest. Only its antennae were
left sticking out. Puddle whined and
nipped at the antennae.

Before Ruby and Harry could do anything, a tall, skinny man wearing a pinstriped suit entered the workshop, holding the hand of a very bored-looking boy.

A murmur of excitement rippled through the room. Mr Gigglesworth had arrived!

The boy yawned.

"Who is he?" Ruby whispered.

"That's Mr Gigglesworth's grandson, Max," Professor Toyjoy whispered. "He gets to play with every toy that's ever made."

"He doesn't look very happy about it," Ruby said. "I'd love to play with every toy that's ever been made."

"You'd soon get bored if playing with toys was your job," Harry told her, "like Max."

"Boredomification is always a problem," Professor Toyjoy muttered. "In order for a toy to win, Max has to like it, and he's very hard to please."

I'd never get bored with toys, Ruby thought, and imagined herself floating in a toy-box boat in a sea of toys.

Mr Gigglesworth made his way through the workshop with a very serious look on his face. He stopped for a few seconds in front of each new toy, and either nodded or shook his head and frowned.

Max shuffled along behind him, yawning and shrugging his shoulders, hardly bothering to glance at each new invention.

Mr Gigglesworth stopped in front of the professor's workbench. "Professor Toyjoy, where is your new toy?" he asked.

"Oh dearie me," Professor Toyjoy sighed sadly. "None of my toys were fantastical enough to present to you today. I fear my toy-making days are over."

The workshop fell silent. The other toy inventors were staring at Professor Toyjoy.

"Woof! Woof! Woof!" Puddle grabbed the Crazy Cuddly Creature's antennae. The little puppy struggled to pull the toy out. The toy was bigger than he was, but he just about managed to drag it across the workshop floor.

"Oh, you naughty puppy – come back!" Ruby cried. She tried to catch hold of Puddle, but missed. She staggered to her feet as the puppy hurled himself at Mr Gigglesworth's grandson, Max.

Thump! Max landed on the floor with Puddle and the Crazy Cuddly Creature on top of him.

"I am so very full of sorryness, Mr Gigglesworth!" Professor Toyjoy exclaimed. "I think we had better leave now. Farebye." The professor hurriedly ushered Ruby, Harry and Puddle towards the workshop door.

"Not so fast!" Mr Gigglesworth thundered. "Come back here!"

Puddle put his tail between his legs and whimpered.

"Oh dear, Puddle," Ruby said. "You've got us in real trouble now!"

Chapter Eight
Toy Joys

"Just look what you've done to
my grandson!" Mr Gigglesworth
boomed.

Ruby, Harry, Puddle and
Professor Toyjoy turned round
slowly. Puddle stood behind Ruby's
legs. Ruby was afraid of what she
might see.

Max was sitting up, hugging the

Crazy Cuddly Creature, with a huge smile across his face.

Ruby's mouth dropped open. So

did Harry's and the professor's.
Puddle's ears pricked up and his tail
started to wag. He ran over to give
Max's cheek a big lick.

Mr Gigglesworth's severe face suddenly softened and his eyes twinkled. "I can hardly believe it!" he gasped. "I've never seen a toy make Max smile before. He loves it."

Mr Gigglesworth turned to the

other toy inventors.

"I hereby declare Professor Toyjoy's creation the winner of the Gigglesworth Toy Competition!" he announced. The other inventors clapped and cheered.

"It's a marvel-fabulo-terrific-acious toy!" Max declared, holding the Crazy Cuddly Creature like a toy aeroplane, and swooping it round his head.

"It can be anything I want it to be. Watch out for the skydiver!"

Mr Gigglesworth caught the

little teddy bear as it flew out of
the creature's pouch. He and his
grandson were both smiling from
ear to ear.

"Hip, hip, hooray!" Ruby and
Harry cheered as Mr Gigglesworth
came over to shake the professor by
the hand.

"Yip! Yip! Yip!" Puddle wagged
his tail so hard that his whole body
waggled.

"What a flabbergastic day!" Professor Toyjoy beamed at Ruby and Harry. "I simply can't thank you enough for your help." Puddle's tail bumped against his legs, and the professor stroked his ears. "And you, Professor Puddle," he added. "You're a proper toy inventor!"

They all laughed, and then Puddle tugged at the hem of Ruby's dress.

"Is it time to go home, Puddle?" she asked.

Puddle barked, and started running in circles round Ruby and Harry. The faces around them started to blur as Puddle ran faster and faster.

"Goodbye, Professor Toyjoy!"
Ruby called. "Make lots more Crazy
Cuddly Creatures. It'll be a bestseller
in the toyshop!"

"Absolutifferously!" Professor
Toyjoy replied, waving them
goodbye. Gigglesworth Toys
seemed to melt away, and Ruby
closed her eyes . . .

***

When Ruby opened her eyes again,
she, Harry and Puddle were sitting
on a picnic blanket next to Grandad's
toy box. It was laid out with plates of
fruit and sandwiches and glasses of
old-fashioned lemonade. Teddy and
Chips were already seated.

"I'm back, Teddy!" Ruby cried,
giving her duck-billed platypus a hug.

Harry switched on his robot, and its eyes flashed.

Puddle ran across the picnic blanket, licked Ruby's and Harry's faces, and ran outside. Ruby and Harry ran to the window to watch him, but the little puppy had already disappeared.

Ruby bent down to pick something up from the doormat. "It's the little teddy from the Crazy Cuddly Creature's pouch," she said, showing it to Harry.

"I can't wait for our next adventure with Puddle," Harry said.

Ruby smiled at her cousin. "Me neither. I hope it rains again soon!"

Can't wait to find out
what Puddle will do next?
Then read on! Here is
the first chapter from
Puddle's third adventure,
Ballet Show Mischief ...

Ballet Show Mischief

"Ladies and gentlemen, the show is about to begin!" Ruby shouted from behind the plush red bedspread hanging across Grandad's living room. She closed her eyes for a moment and imagined a huge theatre filled with people, calling her name.

"Ruby! Ruby!"

She waved to her imaginary fans,

until she realized they sounded like her cousin Harry.

"Ruby! Ruby, can you hear me? What are you doing back there?" he asked.

"It's a surprise." She giggled, and peeked round the bedspread. "Ready?"

"Um, sorry, Ruby, I've got to finish this maze," Harry said, pushing his glasses back in place and burying his nose in a puzzle book.

Never mind, Ruby thought as she ducked back behind the curtain, *the show must go on*. She took a big breath and tugged on her plaits for luck. Her stomach felt as if it was being tickled by fairy wings. She pulled back her pretend curtain.

"Welcome to Ruby's Enchanted Ballet," she said, holding the edges of her wrinkly tutu and curtsying like she'd seen real dancers do. The wall behind Ruby was covered with drawings of rainbows, castles, mountains and forests. Ruby had coloured them all in herself, on separate sheets of paper, and taped them together.

She twirled around on her tiptoes with her arms high above her head. But her socks were slippery. Her legs slid in opposite directions, causing Ruby to accidentally do the splits.

"Ta da!" she sang with her arms outstretched, turning the splits into a part of her dance routine.

"So that's what you've been working on all morning," Harry said, and closed his puzzle book.

Ruby pushed the 'play' button on Grandad's CD player and soft violin music filled the air.

"Now watch me do a spinning top," she said, holding out her tutu and twirling to the music.

"Those are called pirouettes," Harry corrected her, "but I think you hold your arms out like this."
He got up from his chair and spun round on his toes with his arms

curved in front of him, using them to help him whirl round. "Woah! That really makes you dizzy," he said, sitting down again.

"And this is my graceful swan," Ruby said. She balanced on one foot and stuck out her arms like wings.

"The real name for that is an arabesque," Harry said.

"I like my name better," Ruby replied, still on one foot. "How come you know so much about ballet?"

"My parents love watching ballet at the theatre, and sometimes they make me go too," Harry said.

Just then the wind blew the front door open with a BANG! Ruby's pictures were whipped from the wall. They swirled around the living room and finally fluttered to the floor.

A puppy dashed onto Ruby's stage and shook himself, spraying water everywhere.

"Puddle!" shouted Ruby, twirling on her toes in delight.

Every time it rained, Puddle the naughty little puppy appeared and swept Ruby and Harry off on a magical adventure.

"Now that's what I call an entrance," Harry said with a laugh.

Puddle tugged at the curtain until it closed.

"I guess that means my show is

over," Ruby said, taking a sweeping bow.

"But our fun has only just begun!" Harry said, chasing Puddle out into the rain.

***

To find out what happens next,
get your copy of
BALLET SHOW MISCHIEF today!

Magic Carpet Ride

Join Puddle, Ruby and Harry
on their first exciting adventure!

Aziz wants to win
the magic carpet
race so he can be
granted a wish
by the beautiful
princess! Can,
Ruby, Harry and
Puddle help Aziz
to win?

Find out in MAGIC CARPET RIDE...

Puddle
the naughtiest puppy

Ballet Show Mischief

Go on a beautiful ballet adventure
with Puddle, Ruby and Harry.

The children are
whisked away to a
wonderful ballet
show, but the shy
ballerina has stage
fright. The show
must go on! Will
Puddle be able to
find a solution?

Find out in BALLET SHOW MISCHIEF…

Rainforest
Hide and Seek

Have you ever wanted to see a rainforest?

Puddle uses his
magic to take Ruby
and Harry through
a puddle and into an
incredible animal
adventure. Things
keep going missing
in the rainforest
– can Puddle figure
out why?

Find out in RAINFOREST HIDE AND SEEK…

Dragon Dance

Join Puddle, Ruby and Harry on
their new adventure in Chinatown!

Li wants to make
his Grandad proud
by appearing in the
Chinese festival.
Can Puddle and the
children help him
to get Lucky the
dragon to dance?

Find out in DRAGON DANCE...

Magic Mayhem

Ruby and Harry are amazed to find themselves in a medieval castle . . .

. . . when Puddle takes them on their latest adventure! They meet a magician's apprentice who is in deep trouble. He's lost his spell book. Can Puddle save the day?

Find out in MAGIC MAYHEM . . .

Dog Safety

Hi, it's Ruby and Harry again with Puddle! We hope you enjoyed our adventure. Now it's time to find out a little more about real dogs and what they need to be healthy and happy.

So who better to teach us all about our lovely doggy friends than **Dogs Trust** – the UK's largest dog charity? They look after lots and lots of dogs and puppies – and are working very hard to help all dogs to enjoy a happy life in a loving home.

With the help of our friends at **Dogs Trust**, we will learn all about how to stay safe around dogs – so you can enjoy being near them without any worries.

Always remember, Puddle is a magical dog, while real dogs and puppies are living animals who need a lot of care, love and attention.

Stay Safe Around Dogs:

Always follow these six top tips to stay safe around dogs:

- Ask the owner if you can touch their dog.
- Hold out your hand and let the dog sniff you.
- Speak softly to the dog so you don't scare him.
- Pat the dog gently so you don't hurt him.
- Play nicely with the dog.
- Leave dogs alone if they are resting or eating.

Congratulations – you have now learnt about how to stay safe around dogs!

See you next time, when we will be learning all about walking a dog.

Remember, "A dog is for life, not just for Christmas®"
Dogs Trust has 18 Rehoming Centres around the UK and Ireland. To find out more please go to:
www.dogstrust.org.uk
For more fun and games please go to:
www.learnwithdogs.co.uk

Find the Puppy!

Everybody is looking for naughty Puddle. Who will be the one to find him – Ruby, Harry or Max? Follow the lines to find out.

A Muddle of Puddles!

Look closely at the pictures of Puddle.
Can you work out which two puppies
are exactly the same?

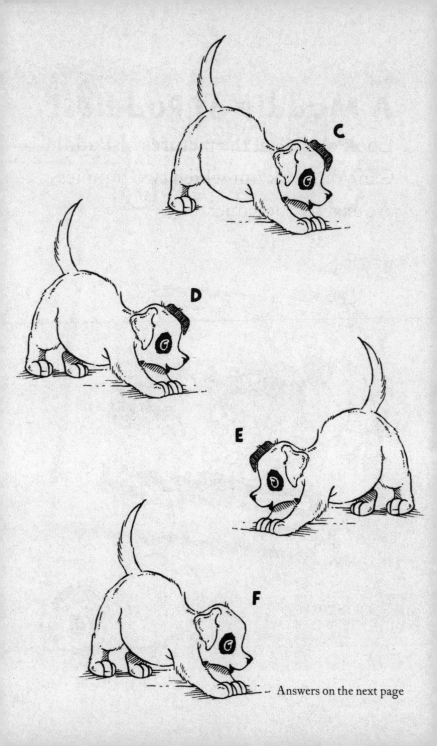

Answers on the next page

Answers to puzzles:
Find the Puppy: Harry finds Puddle
A Muddle of Puddles: B&D are the same

For more magical adventures, come and play with Puddle at

www.puddlethepuppy.com

Use this special code to get extra-special games and free stuff at puddlethepuppy.com

TEDDY